A LOOKIT! BOOK! VOLUME 3

PIRANHA PANCAKES

ZONE OF AUTOGRAPHING

RAY FRIESEN

DON'T EAT ANY BUGS PRODUCTIONS

FIDGET
RAYMOND Q. WONDERFUL
RODERICK
SCRUMPLES
NINCY
TREVOR
THE KING
EGGNER
HORRIBLE BITEY PIRANHA
MELLVILLE THE PENGUIN

BATGUIN
CAPTAIN CAUTIOUS
WILLIAM J. WOOLINGTON III
TBYRD FEARLESSNESS
HOPALONG CASSOWARY
COLONEL HECKINSHAW
GORDON MARMOSETT
SOME CAMEL GUY
FANG
SNAPPER
WRECKS

TABLE *of* CONTENTS

Hello, Person Who Is Reading This Book! I'm Chester Blatherington!

And I'm Robert Bob Robertson. I sure hope you don't get any papercuts!

We're your FABULOUS NARRATORS!

It's our job to explain what's going on. (And sometimes give out bandages...)

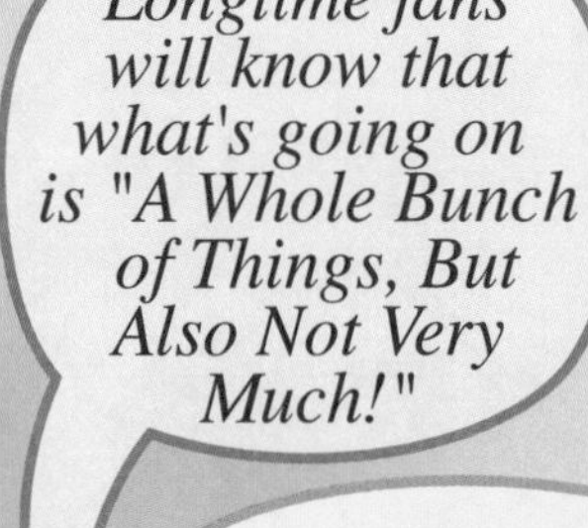

Longtime fans will know that what's going on is "A Whole Bunch of Things, But Also Not Very Much!"
And don't worry, even though you're holding volume 3, you don't need to read any of the other books first.

Although you totally should! (It says in the script I have to say that).
CUPCAKES
DOOM!

I think it's time to bring in the main characters.
Ooh, I love this part!

BOOKWIDE MEETING! All cartoon characters report!
WHANG BANGA BANG KLANG!
get well Please
Aloha! Wuzzup?

Bad news everyone! There's a color shortage! Someone around here has been stealing it all. I'm looking at YOU, Reading Rhino!
You think it was ME? NUH UH! I brought these rainbow suspenders from home!
What about you other mischievious characters, was it any of you guys?

Gee--
Er...
Um...
We didn't steal no colors!
We just borrowed them to make matching 'Bad Characters Club' mood rings. Shiny!
NOT TO BE CONFUSED WITH THE 'NOT VERY GOOD CHARACTERS CLUB"
I THINK I'M A CLEVER CHARACTER...
BLEAH! I'M A VAMPIRE WALRUS!

We're gonna have to shut off the color at the end of this page. If you have any color based jokes, do them now.

What do you mean 'color jokes?'
YEAH?!?
Y'know, stuff like "look how red that red thing is, hahaha!"
That was just pathetic.

So, you're saying we don't have to be printed in color to be funny?

I don't think we said that, but... sure, why not?
Okay guys, it's starting! Prepare yourselves! 3...2...1!

CMYK!

Happy New Year!
You're a very strange person.
WHOA, DADDY-O! FEELS LIKE I'M LIVING IN THE 1950'S! SPIFFY!
I FEEL LIKE I'M LIVING IN THE 2150'S PERSONALLY
HEY! MELLVILLE'S CHEATING!
Hmm? Oops! How embarass-ing!
I got confused since penguins are sorta in black and white anyway? NRG!
There. Happy?
Okay, everybody skedaddle back to your own stories now. If anybody gets eaten by crocodiles or whatever, during their adventures...
I've got bandage strips.
Pfft. Everybody knows the main characters never get hurt.
What? Nobody told us that!
Maybe we're not 'main' enough?

Our first story in this book is 'Um, I Think Your Piranha Are Broken' Starring Raymond Q. Wonderful (the Boy of Wonderfullness) Fidget (his cousin, the responsible one) and Mellville, the Penguiniest Penguin in all the land!
Which land?

Funnily enough, an island: Pellmellia -- part of the Minutae Archepelligo. Chief exports: tourism & cheese ...
Is that important? I hate stories that start with a big map.
YUCITANIA
PELLMELLIA
QUETZL CONGO

You'll just have to read and find out!
So basically, a boy, a girl, a penguin, ADVENTURE. Simple yet effective. Do we have any popcorn?

Shh. It's starting!
Don't shush me!

UM, I THINK YOUR
PIRANHA
ARE BROKEN
AN RQW CARTOON ADVENTURE!
Poke. Wakeup.

Floogilrambthwarg! Morning! Thanks for letting me sleep on your uncomfortable couch you guys! I had a bunch of weird dreams full of exploding cheese. Also chicken ninjas, and pirates were EVERYWHERE!
That wasn't a dream. Those were all the weird people we met in our adventures the past couple days. You invited them over for breakfast, remember?
YARG! We need more maple syrups!
LIBERTY MUSTARD
No, in my dream, they were DIFFERENT pirates and DIFFERENT chicken ninjas.
Can I get some shrimp in my omelette?
All out. Want some orange slices instead?

SO! What's on our schedule for today? I'm in the mood for another exciting adventure!
I'm not! It's been too hectic! I just want to relax on a beach somewhere.
KNOCK NOK.
Who is it?
Singing Telegram Patrol!
Shh! NOBODY'S HERE! No good ever comes from singing telegrams.

KaBlâm!
KNOCK KNO--
Hey! We needed that door!
Oh yeah, I was supposed to tell you guys: Eggner from next door borrowed all your screws and a half bucket of sugar for one of his weird experiments. So, don't touch... anything?
Ahem. King Houngadounga sent us to fetch you at once! He's at the palace!

...Was that a haiku? That doesn't count as singing!

Who sez we have to rhyme in a traditional fashion? Pfft.
Ooh, pancakes! Mind if we barge in?

Hiya Kingy! Wassup?
That's not the correct way to speak to a king! You will address me as 'Your Highness!'

I don't think you're tall enough to be a 'highness'. Let's compromise with a 'what's up, your majesty'?

Nah, I'm not very majestic either. There's that famous dancing video of me all over the internet to prove it...
Okay, just bow, and then curtsy, and then say 'Hello Julius P. Houngadounga, your kingitude.'
Hiya Julie! Sup?

I gots a secret mission for you. So... Go do it.

You can't order us around like that!

Do you SEE the CROWN?

I'm not even one of your subjects.

In that case, you'll want to obey me ESPECIALLY, so as not to cause an international incident!

Was that too mean? I'm trying to rule through a combination of Love and Fear, but I haven't quite gotten the dosages right yet.

Love and fear-- Don't they combine to make respect? Yeah, we don't respect you.

Would you respect me if I gave you... CANDY?!?
Totally!
Woo!
YAY!

So anyway, I have a mission that needs doing, and you guys are the only ones around here who actually listen to me.

Well, the Singing Telegram people do too, but they're getting more and more snippy. And expensive.
I should really just get a new cellphone.
My old one got eaten by a sheep, and my warranty thingy is really confusing.

Anyway! It's my birthday next week, and I need you guys to go to all my royal friends in neighboring countries and deliver the party invitations.

I'm turning old, so I better get alot of presents to help me cope.
Why can't you just mail the invites?

The Pellmellian Postmaster and I are having a feud. He's locked himself in the post office and won't let anybody buy any stamps until I give in to his demands.
What does he want?

Pfft. I don't even remember. Buncha stupid stuff. So! Here's your bag-o-mail, and your Diplomatic Immunity Visa.
Flash that Diplomatic Immunity pass at anybody here in the Minutae Islands, and they'll have to do what you say.
Wow! I had no idea Pellmellia was such an important and powerful country for that sort of thing to work!

Sorta. We all share the same submarine for our imperial navies, and it's my turn to use it this month.
So we can use this visa to get free plane flights, hotels and food?

Yup! So don't go abusing its priveleges!
Sure... Hee hee hee.

MEANWHILE, IN A SOMEWHERE ELSE TYPE PLACE, SOME VILLAINS OF THIS STORY ARE BEING INTRODUCED!

This meeting of the Loyal Order of the Nocturnal Owls of Midnight will now begin-commence. BRETHREN!
And Sisteren!
Yes, thank you Nincy.
Why is it so dark in here?
Because owls LOVE the dark!
They do? No we don't. You're thinking of bats.
OWLS DON'T LOVE BATS.

Who wants Mice Krispy Treets?

MOM! You're ruining the whole cryptic club atmosphere I've got going on!
Thanks Mrs. Hootinanny!

WAIT, YOU GUYS ARE ALL ACTUALLY OWLS? I THOUGHT... UM.

Owls and Honorary Owls.

I SHOULD GO.

And if you tell anyone of the secrets you learned here, you will be silenced! To DEATH!

Hmph. Well, now that all the interruptions are out of the way--
Hey, where's your bath-room?

Down the hall, to the left. But you're not allowed to use it. It's full of a piano. Now, as I was saying--
So why did you call this meeting, Roderick?

BECAUSE! Too long have we owls been oppressed!
Have we? I don't think so. If anything, we haven't been oppressed enough.

Look at us! We're endangered species! Forced to carry mail for ungrateful wizards!

You're thinking of those books Rodj, we don't really do that. There are no such things as wizards.

Well, Scrumples here works for the post office! And his assistant manager is an amateur magician, so that's pretty close...
It's not so bad. I get Tuesdays and holidays off, and all the stamps I can eat. Plus, I told you, it's only temporary. I'm trying to become an actor.

I say it's time to take back what's ours!
You mean our lunch money? Dude, that was in the fourth grade. Let it go.

No, I mean we should try to conquer the world!
HAHAHAHAH!
hee hee hee hee!

Dude! You sound like some kinda lame cartoon super-villain!

We never even HAD the world, how could we take it back?
I had a bucket once, it was kinda world-shaped.

I'm serious! I think if we join together, combine all our skills and talents--
What talents?

I can juggle.
I can whistle with my eyes closed.

Look dude, to be super-villains, you need all kinds of stuff. A secret HQ, booby-traps for the heroes that try to stop you, evil plans... etcetera!

I got all that stuff! Come down to my basement, I have some-thing awesome to show you...

It's not your washing machine again, is it? To be honest, I wasn't all that impressed the first time.

BACK TO THESE GUYS:
Who knows how long we're gonna be away adventuring, so pack light, just bring the essentials.
I'm gonna go check on something else that might be useful...
Hi Eggner! Since you're our wacky mad scientist next door neighbor, I was wondering if--
What do you mean "Mad Scientist"?
I'm a normal scientist! Just look how normal my lab coat is!

That's not a lab coat. It's a disco suit.

Really? That would explain a bunch of the giggling that goes on behind my back...
Not all of it, but yeah, some.

Hey, when you dubbed me 'mad' did you mean angry or crazy? BECAUSE I'M NOT CRAZY! RAWR!

Your haircut would beg to differ.
What? Oh! This isn't my normal hairstyle. I just keep getting electrocuted alot lately.

ANNNNYWAAY...
I was wondering if you had any awesome new inventions we could borrow?
Y'know, the kind of thing that at first seem useless, but then have a really practical use that saves us from whatever dangers we encounter?

Nope!
Nope?!? That's pretty much the exact opposite answer from what I wanted!

I don't really design stuff, my dear penguin. My work is hypothetical. Do you even READ my BLOG?
I tried, but your blog is really boring. So, well, hmm. I guess this visit was pretty useless.
CHEESE IDENTIFICATION CHART

Gee, sorry. Tell that to Heisenberg!
I don't know who that is, or want to.

Wait! I feel totally guilty now! I guess I have something for you after all!
Yay!
My lucky Science Hammer. You use it for hammering stuff in a scientific way. It means a lot to me.
...Um, great! Thanks! Well... bye!
Toodles.
NTRANSE
...
Disco boogie!
I'm back! Everybody packed? Got those weird clothes thingies you're so fond of?
Yup! I've got a bag full of pajamas, toothpaste and socks.
And my satchel is full of comic books and chocolate! LET'S VAMOOSE!

HEY DAD?!?
We're gonna go out of the country for a couple days or a week or three!
Okay! You, your cousin, and your pet penguin have fun! Try not to get eaten by crocodiles!
Pet Penguin? ME? Pfft. More like I have two pet humans.
Taking care of humans is a big responsibility you know.

So, how should we get to the airport?
Taxi?
Nah. Leave this to the Diplomatic Immunity Visa and me!
AND SO--
Messrs. Contraption and Gyrocopter, Proprietors
STEAMPUNK-ATORIUM
3 jetpacks please! Make it snappy!
SNAP!
SNAP!
SNOP!
SNAP!
SNAP!
SNAP!
Aw, snap.

I think it was farther to walk to the jet-pack store than it was to the airport, we could have just--
Shh. You're ruining it.
PELLMELLIAN NTERNATIONAL AIRPORT AND USED CAR DEALERSHIP
TICKETS
SNACKS $27
Hello Mr. Airport dude! 3 plane tickets please! Heck, just give us the whole plane. And someone to drive it around. Make it... quickly!
Uh, ok.
QWIK!
TROPICANADA
YUCITANIA
PELLMELLIA
QUETZL CONGO
SAHARA
Francylvania! Land of snooty vampires! We're sure to have a spooky adventure here!
COUNT BITEY'S CHATEAU, FRANCYLVANIA

Ooh!
Hmf.
Hiya, your Countlyness! Got a letter for ya!

Neat! Thanks!

Okay, Bye.

That's it? Aren't you gonna have your vampire minions attack us?
Or challenge us to a truffle hunting contest, our penguin versus your Finest Fire Pig?
Or have us comb your hair since you can't use mirrors?

Nah. S'Cool. G'wan, beat it.

Well that adventure was a big bust.
I thought it went well. Very organized!

Hey pilot, What island are we flying over now?
Yucitania.

Hmm... Sure are a lot of beaches and palm trees on it...

Yup! It's a tropical paradise! My brother lives there, runs the snorkel and sombrero rental store. He eats shrimp tacos for lunch every day! The lucky jerk.

Fidget, wouldn't it be more... efficient if our mail delivery squad split up?

Well...

Great! I'll take one of these letters to the Yucitanian El Presidente, you guys take the rest, we'll meet back later!
Okay, I guess we could do most of the work...
Let's have the pilot land, and--

No time! I'll take a parachute and jump!
We're not high enough for your chute to have time to deploy!

Okay, I'll take the jetpack as well.

FWOOSH!

Hello palm tree! Thanks for help with my landing!
Wait! Too bendy! TOO BENDY!

AUGH!
Sprango!

JOES DISCOUNT FISHATORIUM
Joes DISCOUNT FISH A TORIUM

Crash!

Hey! What did that window ever do to you?
Mrg. IT GOT IN MY WAY.

Grnk. Is this a seafood restaurant or an aquarium?

Both! Welcome to Joe's Discount Fishatorium! D'ya want a pet, or a meal?
Both. But first I'd like some bandages, I'm feeling a little... head trauma-y.

Hey, boss? It's me. No, TREVOR. Yeah, I'm at work. No, I think I found a hero-type guy we can test 'The Trap' on!

Nah, he crashed thru the front window. It was really cool and dramatic, he's a main character sort of person for sure. Yeah, I'll hold.
dum de dum ta dum da da...

SO! LATER, AT A SECRET HEADQUARTERS PLACE--

Hey! Whoever you are! Penguin guy! WAKE UP! We're your NEW arch-nemesesses! THE OWLS!
That's our evil organization's codename? SHEESH. At least tell me it's a secret code, right? O.W.L.S.? Owls-With-Laser-Sharks?
ZZZZZzzzzz...
WASH O CO

Znurk? Where am I?
Our DUNGEON of DOOM!
It's your mom's basement.
BASEMENT of DOOM!
You can't just afix 'doom' to the end of something and make it cool.
YES I CAN!

I don't want any doom. I want pancakes.

I suppose I could go whip up some batter. We've got a waffle iron, if you'd prefer-

DON'T YOU DARE COOK THE PRISONER ANY DELICIOUS TREATS!

ZZZ
AW MAN! The prisoner fell asleep again! How are we supposed to explain our evil plans NOW?
Super-villains don't ALWAYS have to explain their plans.

It's TRADITION! We do this by the book!
What are our evil plans anyway?
HOW 2 VILLIAN

Yeah, you never told us!
It's not right, telling your archenemy before your loyal minions!

FINE! Our plan is... to do EVIL THINGS! EVILLY!

That is the vaguest plan I've ever heard.
It leaves lots of room for interpretation though...
I think--

No one cares what you think. WAKE UP THE PRISONER!

Snif. I care what I think.
I care too! Unless you think about boring things.

I can't reach! My cute lil arms are too stumpy!

Show some INITIATIVE you doof!

SMEK!
SMEK!
SMEK!
Ow.
Hey! Thbxth! What?

Chomp Chomg.

Mmm! Fish-licious! Excellent room service you got around here! What was that, perch? Pike? Something with p...

You want P-Fish, do you? BEHOLD! THE SUPER BITEY PIRANAH!
Where?
Down here, dummy.

I can't see them too well from way up here...
So you want a closer look, huh?
Or glasses.

TREV! Release the Rope!

Okay.

Eep!
Gravity!
SPLASH CO™
INFLATO - KIDDIE. POOOOOOL™

SPLASH!

AUGH! Shriek!

Evil Bitey Fish! Irony! Help!

Um... I think your piranha are broken, nothing's happening. What's the deal here?

Are you filming this? Am I being pranked?

Trev! YOU FOOL! I told you not to buy the piranha from Joe's Discount Fishatorium! They're obviously just goldfish with plastic vampire fangs!

Dude, chillax, you're getting spit in my face. I get a 7% employee discount from Joe's! And we can still return them!

Burp. No you can't.

BOOOOHOO! I can't do anything right! I'm a miserable excuse for a super-villain, nobody hates me!
Aww, there there! We're your friends! Of course we hate you!
We hate you with love!
Snif. Thanks guys. I guess I just gotta believe in myself, be confident!
We didn't say that. Don't go crazy.
I'm not CRAZY! I'M MAD! MWAHAHA AHAHA!
See? You got that evil laughter down pat!
Thanks! You should see my evil hiccups!
We've got a little bit of time left before me and Trev's lunch breaks are over. The prisoner is still tied up, let's--
No I'm not!

I used my lucky hammer to cut the ropes, and now I'm totally escaping! Toodles!

Run!
Run!
Run!
Escape!

Well,

Roderick Kenneth Hootinanny! Language!
Ooo! You gonna get in troublllllle!

MOM! What are you doing in my Basement of Doom?
Laundry.

What a bunch of weirdos. Oh well, owls well that ends well.
Now: I'm gonna find that beach!

My penguin senses detect that the ocean is... THAT WAY!
Although, this is an island, so I guess I could point in any direction and that would be true...

A COUPLE HOURS LATER, I DUNNO, MAYBE THREE?
pant *pant* *pant*
Hey Mellville! Where have you been?
LIFEGARD

Urg. Jungle. Swamp. Mountain. More swamp. More jungle. I hate this island. What are you guys doing here? Finished already? Can we go home?

Nah, You took the Diplomatic Immunity Visa with you, so the pilot wouldn't fly us around anymore. Unless we paid him. And since the King didn't give us his royal credit card...

Actually, I do have King Houngadounga's credit card, but that's a different story entirely...

Well, now you're back, we can commandeer a helicopter or something, and visit the next country!

Where you wanna go? This letter is for the Emir of Quetzlcongo -- he lives in a palatial tree fort surrounded by lost diamond mines filled with man-eating rhinocermoose.
Sounds exciting!
Nah. What else you got?

How about this letter, for the Queen of Boomerangatang? I think today is their annual Sheep-Flinging-Festival, we could all wear cork-hats and get kangaroo-cheese quesadillas!
What is it with you mammals and your fascination with dairy products?

Well, you pick then, you're the one with the Diplomatic Visa that will get us there!
Ooh, I hope we get to travel in a submarine! That would be awesome!
Hang on-- my pockets are empty...
...I must have dropped it...
brbl sigh grg.

Hey, what's this?
Mrg? MRG! Hfeee Hefee fhee! Gargle.
SOAP
Roderick, you're foaming at the mouth again...

How are we supposed to deliver the letters now?
By relaxing? Crazy, but it just might work!
We could try sticking the letters in the mail...

We can't buy any stamps! The Pellmellian Postmaster General won't let anyone--
We're not in Pellmellia.

Yes! We Sell Postcards
YUCITANIA POST OFF.
POST

Hello! 200 stamps please! Here's my credit card, which is totally mine.
CHANGE OF ADDRESS
¡WOW!

May I see some ID Mr... King Houngadounga?
Of course not! King's never carry ID! We're too important.

Then how do I KNOW you're a king? Where's your crown? You know, you look kinda familiar...

You've probably seen me on TV, I'm very famous. SERVANTS?
SNOP!

Gasp! YOUR HIGHNESS!

Aw, shucks! Thanks! But I'm not tall enough to be a higness... Or am I? SERVANTS!

Tadaa!
Hup!

Ooooh! SOOOOOOOO Majestic!

Okay everybody! Stamp licking party!
Count me out. I don't have enough spit. I'm gonna wander across the street in search of liquids ...and tacos.
Mr. Post Owl-- do you have any friends who can help us with this licking project?

Why yes... YES I DO!

Hey, Roderick? It's me. SCRUMPLES. No- yeah. come on down to the post office. Bring your tongue...
SNEAK...

AND THUS:
LICK
LICK
LICK
LICK
LICK

What are all these envelopes for exactly?

The return address says "King Houngadounga Po Box Seven Pellmellia". Some sort of code?
We had that King in here earlier, real nice guy, very regal. Not like these modern princesses with all their...tiaras.

These are invitations, the 17th is the King's birthday. We're sending these to the rulers of all the other countries.

Do you mean to say, that next week, all of the thrones around here are going to be... EMPTY?

Yup!

I think my plan on how to take over the world just got a little less vague...

Mwah Ha Ha! HA! MWAH HA HA HA!
Hee hee hee hee hee!
Giggle! Guffaw!
Har har har! Snort!

MwaHaHa! CoughaBlough. Hink! Hink! Hink!
That's some great diabolical hiccupping, boss.
And so, I found a fancy drink, all the invitations got mailed, everything was perfect, and everybody lived happily ever after! Hurray!
THE END
Wait, is that seriously The End? What about the birthday party, and the owl's world dominationing?
I thought it all tied together pretty nicely. Those ideas will just have to wait for future books I guess.

So it's really a 'To Be Continued'?
Maybe. Not really. Who knows?

Soooo... Now what's happening?
We've got several smaller stories next, all about 10 pages. These are all those characters you saw earlier, who really each live in their own self containted universe.

I Wish I had my own universe! I'd fill it with Awesome Things. Like... lots of money, superheroes, food, motorcycles, cowboys monsters, maybe even a sheep.
Actually, the next stuff has all those things!

What an amazing coincedence. NOT.
Coming up: periodic updates from Captain Cautious's Blog, the Vampire Dinosaurs on Motorcycles, and Colonel Heckinshaw's TV show "Cooking With Danger!"

Well then, let's stop talking, ...and start reading!

WWW.CAPTAINCAUTIOUS.COM BLOG

PLEASE WIPE YOUR DIGITAL FEET.

Name:
"Captain" Prancibald Evil-Dooer-Smasher Cautious (Really, that's what's on my birth certificate)

College: Yvonne's Haircutting Academy

Family Business: Super Heroing

Current Job: Butler/BodyGuard/ Best friend to Billionaire Sheep

I thought I'd start posting some of my experiences on the internet for two reasons: They're interesting, and I'm scared of papercuts.

March 19 8:07 PM
Today, my boss, William J. Woolington III, the world's richest sheep bought a giant novelty checkbook. Like they give you when you win a gameshow? He feels the enormousness better fits his super-rich persona. I have to carry it around, it's quite heavy. He wrote two checks today, one for 50 cents to buy gum, and one for $200 for a red and blue neck-tie set (he wants to wear them both at the same time so they'll "Be in 3D". I told him people need special red and blue glasses for that kind of 3D to work,and so he bought a truckload to hand out to anyone looking at him).

I asked for a blank check I could take to the chiropractor, since carrying the darn things were causing me excessive spinal cord discomfurture, and he laughed in my face. There was spittle. I felt the need to boil my head afterwards. I HATE GERMS.
0 Comments

March 26 6:15 PM
Mr. The Third told me how he got so rich today – I knew he didn't earn it, he's way too lazy. Apparently, his father, Billy Woolington Jr, worked in the mail room at the corporate offices of McLarry's – the ridiculously unhealthy fast food chain. One day, McLarry's was merging with another company, Drive By Mortuary. Important documents whizzed in and out of the mail room for weeks, and Billly acquired the habit of opening them, and changing some of the words and names. When all was said and done, he was CEO of the combined company! He had other business skills than sneakiness too. Billy left a ridiculously large fortune to his son, who is determined to spend it all. He bought the letter W today, no one else can use now it without paying him royalties.

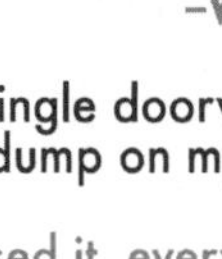

1 Comment
Oh dear, I'm gonna owe him a bunch of money...
–**Wolfgang Wooster,** Wyoming

April 1 11:11AM
I got fooled today. Every single doorway in the mansion contained a bucket of water poised to dump on my head. So I went back to bed.

1 Comment
Hee hee! You missed it, every single jar also had a springy snake in it ready to jump out at you! Spoilsport!
–**William J. Woolington III,** 3rd Floor Breakfast Nook

April 17 3:03 AM

Batguin. In addition to myself, and the roving construction crew and food court workers, we also have a Batguin. We don't know what he is exactly, we found him in a box of cereal, he is very wiggly. His job seems to be getting mud over EVERYTHING, eating all the sugar, and hiding all of the mansion's lamps in a secret cubbyhole somewhere. Today, he opened up a lemonade stand, which just sold lemons with straws stuck in them. He made $17,000.

1 Comment
It was hot today after all. Who told you about my lampy paradise?
–**Batguin,** The Attic, North Astronomy Tower, Bellfry

"AND LO, THE HEAVENS SHALL SPILL FORTH WITH LASERS, AND ALL MANNER OF GIANT MONSTER ROBOT THINGS SHALL TROMP UPON THE EARTH, AND YEA, THE CHOCOPOCALYPSE SHALL BE UPON US!"
--CRAZY JIMMY, DISCOUNT PROPHET
FGGF
FOODGOOD
GASFAST
ALiens
Robots
monsters
MINI MART
zombies

VAMPIRE DINOSAURS on MOTORCYCLES

AUGH! Ghosts!

Don't worry! I'm the ghost of you! From the future! I've traveled back in time to keep you company!

Vrooom Vroooom Vroooooooooomidy Vroooomvroooom

That's better! Let there be light!

Hee hee. I'm so witty.

You guuuys!
I can't fit through the automatic doors!

CRUNCH!

Ding! That's better!
SMASH!

Hee hee. Wrecks, you're so destructiony!
Hello Miss! My name is Snapper! Three Slurpo-ice drinks please!

Really? Um... What flavor?
SLURPO

BLOOD!
Blood.
Butter-scotch!

GLARE
Oh right, we discussed this. I'm not very cool. Blood-erscotch?

Sluuuuurp!
Sluurpedy!
Sluurp!

Gulp!

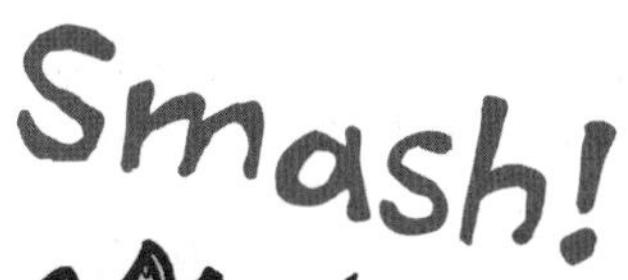
Smash!

You da Man-A-Saurus, Fang!

Ooh! My turn!
Smosh!

I prolly shoulda drinked it first.
ARG! Brainfreeze!

Your brain's the size of a walnut, it should only last a second!

Well, thanks Amanda! You're one of the few places with enough electricity to still make freezy drinks, so we'll be back!

Okay! Thanks for not eating me!

Sure! We're good guys!

We're not evil? But-- we're vampires! And not the sparkly kind!
We're complex, conflicted individuals.
I'm not.

Um, I'm stuck again.
I don't see how, that door is now your exact shape!
Hey, who's over there by our motorcycles?

Ahoy!

RAWR! Don't touch our bikes!
Who are you JERKS?

Wereshark! No autographs, PLEASE.
WHACK!
Oops!
Oooooooh!
Hee heee hee!

We were just taking a little spin up the canal on our boaty boats, and thought we'd come hassle you!
So, where are your training wheels?
Snicker!
GRRR!
You think you're so tough!
Bring it!
FLICK! FLICKEDY! FLICK!
SHING!
Put that tiny switchblade away, I'm gonna give 'em my Serrated Smile!
GLAAAH. 30 Rows of Chompers, baby!
I've just got the one row, but they're each the size of your face!
Urmp!

Whatchoo got? Bring it! I have Plus Five Moustache Power!
Guys! Violence never solved anything!

It didn't?

Nah! Why don't we have a race?
We could go down to the beach, Bikes vs. Boats, Surf vs Turf!

And so, they do:

Ooh, we are so gonna win! You guys are gonna be all 'Boo Hoo, we're so sad!'
Nice smack talk Wrecks.

Wait, if we win, what's the prize?
Gloating Rights!

ThreeTwoOneGO!
VROOM!
Hey! We weren't ready!

VEER!
SPLATCH!
Hey!
Hee hee hee!
Help! I've fallen and I can't get up!

PATTA! PATTA! PATTA!
Ptui. I think I just lost.
Tra la la... Huh? Crud! I forgot about the race!

BVBROOM!
HAR
POOH
That's not good...
HARPOONY WHIZ!
SHOOT!
POW!
WUNK!

WHIZ!
WHIZ!
WHIZ!
EXPLODE!

I've been tree'd.

VROOM!
Zooom
FIRE!
FOONT!

WHIP!

GRR!

JAM!

CRUNCHSPLODE!

Yipe!

THAT WAS MY FAVORITEST BIKE! RAWR!
Hey! Get off! You're cheating!
HISS! No rule against cheating!

Oh good, cuz we've been cheating this whole time.

MOOOOON

OBSCURE!

POOF!
Whu?

What's happening?
I think they just lost their werewolf-shark powers.
FLOP FLOPPITY FLOP

Stupid moon covering clouds.

I WIN! GLAR!
Help!

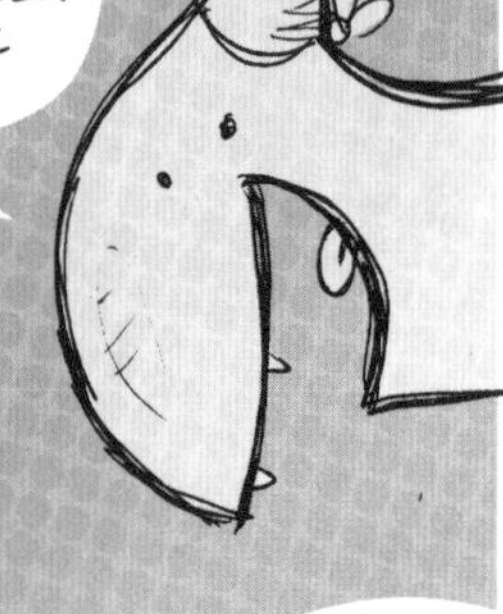

I could bake us some celebratory muffins!

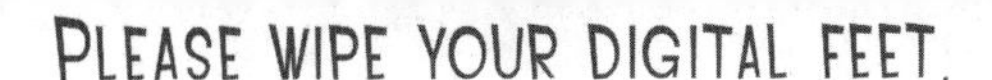

April 21st 4:44 PM
Tax day. I keep all my W2's in an organized pile, and so merely had to fill out a quick spreadsheet. Mr The Third's finances are so complicated, he had to hire every accountant on the eastern seaboard, and they still couldn't figure it out. Apparently William J. doesn't keep any receipts. He finally ended up sending every single member of the IRS on an all expense paid cruise to Alaska, where I think he's hoping they'll get eaten by polar bears....
0 Comments

May 3 8:56 PM
I bought new gloves today. They're thicker than my old pair, and felt weird the first time I wore them, but now they feel fine and my old ones feel weird.

2 Comments
Visit SpamaLamaDingDong.com for aLL your GLOEV NeEDS!
–Spamvertiser 3000, THe TwitterNETs, U-S-HAY!

No. – **Captain Cautious,** Right Here

May 12th 7:12 AM
You know what the suckiest part about being invulnerable is? Haircuts. I pride myself on having a fashionable hairdoo, but it's nearly impossible to maintain, since when you try to cut my follicles, you end up breaking the scissors. I usually go to 'KoganKlipz' – that stylist with adamantium shears, but there's a sign on the door saying she's been sent on a secret mission somewhere classified (probably Atlantis again). In the mean time, I'm eating lots of carrots, and hoping to acquire laser vision, and maybe trim my own hair with the help of some mirrors.
Current Mood: Scruffy/frustrated. Scruffstrated...
0 Comments

May 29th 7:12 PM
My birthday. Mr The Third invited every superhero he could think of to a party in my honor! I only know two of them: Jeremy the Impressive, (my cousin, who I don't like very much) and FalconFace, the girl who can transform her face into any kind of falcon. They seem to be having a great time drinking all my imported honey cola, and spilling stuff on the lovely couch. I tried to make small talk to El Shrinko, but he's an inch tall, and only speaks Spanish in a very squeaky voice... I'm writing this post as I hide in the broom cupboard, waiting for everyone to leave.
1 Comments
You don't like me? I'm telling Granma!
JEREMY THE IMPRESSIVE, MOONBASE ONE

May 29th 11:12 PM
UPDATE 'Indestructible Irwin" and "The Nightmare Ninja TM", a couple supervillains crashed the party, and an epic fight broke out. I got knocked unconsciou by a falling chandelier. When I came to, the entire mansion has has been destroyed, so it appears everyone has allready gathered their coats,apes and such, and gone back to wherever it is they call home.
0 Comments

May 30th 6:12 AM
Mr. The Third has had the entire mansion rebuilt in just 6 hours. Probably cost a pretty penny. He decided instead of regular doors, to redo everything in trap doors, so now everything is revolving book cases and secret staircases. I can't find the kitchen.

1 Comments
It's next to the secret submarine base. Go thru the haunted library, and climb the non-fake rope ladder.
–William J. Woolington, Secret Kitchen Alpha

June 11 4:57 PM
Batguin won a tour of the Crunchy Cereal Company factory today, and chose William J as his plus one. They had magical, Wonkaesqaue adventures. I stayed home and vacuumed.

HELLO! COLONEL HECKINSHAW HERE! WELCOME TO MY TV SHOW COOKING WITH DANGER!
FOOG IT'S HOT!
I'M GORDON MARMOSETT, EXECUTIVE MONKEY PRODUCER.
AS REGULAR VIEWERS KNOW, WE TRAVEL ALL OVER THE WORLD IN SEARCH OF DELICIOUSNESS.
TODAY, WE'RE IN SAHARIA, RAIDING TOMBS AND WHATNOT TO TRY AND FIND COLONEL PHAROAH'S KENTUCKY FRIED SCARABS!
WITH 11 MUMMIFIED HERBS AND SPICES! MMM!
THIS WILL BE OUR TOUGHEST AND SWEATIEST ASSIGNMENT EVER.
LET'S CHECK THE LOCAL MARKETPLACE-BAZAAR.
YOU'RE BIZZARE!
HEY! WHERE IS EVERYBODY? THIS PLACE SHOULD BE FILLED WITH ALL MANNER OF ARABIAN CHARM! WHAT'S THE DEAL?
WE LOST ALL OUR FOOT TRAFFIC ONCE THE MALL OPENED UP.
WELL, LOOKY THERE!
MALL
DING!
AHHHH! AIR CONDITIONING!
LET'S CHECK OUT THE FOOD COURT! THOUGH I DOUBT THEY'LL HAVE ANY SCARABS...
SCARABS
UM...
SCARABS! KENTUCKY FRIED
SCARABS!
WE'LL EDIT THIS OUT SO OUR QUEST WILL SEEM HARDER.

HELLO MUMMY! TWO BUCKETS OF SCARABS, PLEASE!
NO, NO HONEY MUSTARD.
HMM... NOPE. THESE ARE ALABAMA FRIED. ONLY 8 SPICES.
CRONCH. CHOMP.
AUGH! THBBX! SANDSTORM!
MY CONTACT LENS!

OKAY, SO NOW IT'S GOT NINE OF THE RIGHT SPICES, BUT IT'S STILL NOT SPICEY ENOUGH! PTUI!

WHAT ARE THE PROPER HERBS USED IN KENTUCKY FRIED SCARABS?
I'LL CHECK THE RECIPE HIEROGLYPHIC TABLET WE GOT FROM THAT MUSUEM.

YOU ROBBED A MUSEUM?
OH NO, I TRADED THE NIGHT SECURITY GUARD A T-REX SKULL FOR IT. HE'S THE ONE WHO STOLE IT.

WAS IT THE T-REX SKULL I GAVE YOU FOR YOUR BIRTHDAY?
NO... IT WAS A DIFFERENT ONE?

OKAY, NO. 1 -- WAVY LINES. THAT EITHER MEANS NUTMEG, OR CINNAMON. POSSIBLY WATER...
NO. 2 - HUMMUS, OR YOU CAN SUBSTITUTE SALAD DRESSING. NO. 3 CHICKPEAS. NO. 4 FROGS.
NO. 5 SHREDDED PAPYRUS BITS. NO. 6 EMBALMING FLUID. NO. 7 SEASONAL FRUITS.
OOH! LIKE DATES?
GORDON, WE CAN DISCUSS YOUR SOCIAL LIFE LATER.
NO. 8 GOLDEN ANKHS (TO TASTE).
NO. 9 SANDY SAND.
NO 10 PAPRIKA--
YOINK!
HEY! I WAS TRANSLATING THAT! BANDIT! THIEF! HELP!
MWA HA HA! COUGH! HA HA!
PUTT! PUTT! PUTT! PUTT! PUTT!
NOW I AM SO TOTALLY IN THE MOOD FOR A FRUIT SMOOTHIE.
TAXI!
YUS?
FOLLOW THAT GUY! HURRY!
HOKAY.
VROOM!
THAT'S TOO FAST. YOU'VE PASSED HIM.
Put Put Put

Sorry, I'm excited! Also, I've had nothing but energy drinks all day.
You should try some of my homemade energy gumbo sometime.
How much do we owe you?
14 Money's Please.
Can you make change for a $100 travelers check?
Nope!
I'm not giving you an $86 tip for a 2 minute ride!
Hmm... I've got an idea...
There you are Gordon! I noticed -- hey, where'd you get the fancy new head clothes?
I don't want to talk about it.
Right. Well! I noticed the bandit had a golden eye tatooed on his knuckle.
That must mean he's a member of Ollie Babba's criminal syndicate! So! All we need to do is stumble around this desert, find thier secret hideout, disguise ourselves as ghosts or mummies or vampires to frighten the guards. We sneak inside, defeat the 40 thieves, each of which is highly trained in a different martial art such as fist-kicking. Then we retrieve the stolen tablet, blow up the building somehow, escape, and fry ourselves up some tasty scarabs! What do you say to that?
RING! RING!
I say hold on a second... Hello? Uh huh. Right.

WHO IZZIT?
THE TEEVEE NETWORK. THEY SAY WE DON'T HAVE THE BUDGET FOR ANY OF THAT COOL STUFF.
OH.
IN FACT, WE'VE EVEN ALREADY RUN OUT OF TIME.
STAGE THREE
SCUTTLE
SO WHAT DO WE DO? HOW DO WE END THIS EPISODE? WE DIDN'T...
SCUTTLE
SCUTTLE
SCUTTLE
SCUTTLE
EW. DON'T EAT ANY BUGS!
CRUNCH
JOIN US NEXT TIME WHEN WE'LL BE IN MEGA-KYOTO, IN SEARCH OF POISONOUS SUSHI!
AND ANTIDOTE SASHIMI!
THE END

WELCOME TO MY BLOG

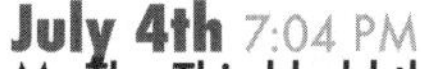

July 4th 7:04 PM

Mr The Third held the world's largest barbecue today, he invited Every Single Person in the United States. The logistics involved to figure out everyone's air travel was very complicated I spent days on the phone with JetGreen, and finally Mr The Third bought every airport there is, just because the customer service representative was being snippy. The tofu hot dogs were delicious-ish, but the soda left something to be desired. Sigh. I miss my Belgian Honey Cola.

1 Comment

Where are the napkins?
–**Wolfgang Wooster,** Condiments Table

July 22nd 4:15 PM

Visited the San Diego Comic Con, Mr. The Third bought one of every comic book ever made, and now has the Most Impressive Collection Ever.

1 Comment

It turns out I'm missing Skullman #26. DARNIT.
–**William J. Woolington III,** On top of the pile of comic books

November 15th. 7:04 PM

Woah. Hi guys. Sorry it's been so long since the last update. I've been reading every comic book in the world except one out loud to Mr. The Third, and lost track of time. I got quite good at doing the voices. He then donated them all to a local school, which built a very impressive fort out of them. Librarians are good architects.

O Comments.

December 24th 11:12 AM

We got kicked out of the mansion, Mr. The Third is broke. Once the IRS got back from Alaska, (well, about half of them, and a fat polar bear wearing a tie and glasses) – they concluded Mr The Third actually went bankrupt months ago, (what with his horrible spending habits and all), and we are now homeless, and living on the streets. It's not as much fun as it sounds. My fingers are crossed for one of those Christmas miracles you hear so much about.

O Comments

December 25th 8:15 PM

Went to Grandma's house, took best shower of my life. Opened presents – socks and underwear, neither of which were particularly miraculous. Grammy said I could sleep on the couch no problem, but I'd rather show solidarity with my friends. Plus, Grandma's couch is made out of cabbage and spoons or something, it's really uncomfortable. I refuse to let my beard stubble be photographed.

O Comments

December 28th 4.56 PM

Scrubbed our dumpster top to bottom, made a lovely casserole out of stale donuts.

2 Comments

How are you updating this blog? We have no computer. –**William J. Woolington**

My gloves get hifi-scifi-wifi. How are YOU getting internet?

January 1st 9:18 AM

A New Years Day Miracle! Even though all of his stuff has been repossessed, apparently, Mr The third still owns the rights to the letter W! We got a phone call from the International Alphabet Commssion, who sent him a check for 14 million dollars for all the DoubleYouing they did last year! The banks aren't open, so we'll have to wait and cash it on Tuesday.

Boo! BooHoo Hoooo! Wah!
What? Are you ...crying? These comics aren't emotiony!
Are you kidding? Captain Cautious triumphed, Colonel Heckinshaw never got to cook, the dinosaurs' bikes broke! It was the most moving piece of graphic novelage I've ever seen! BAWW!
You crybaby.
You unfeeling robot!
Woah, what's happening?
The book is rotating. We got a memo about this, remember?
No. Is it a California thing? Earthquakes?
Kinda: the Tbyrd stories always go longways.
Who's stupid idea was that?

TBYRD FEARLESSNESS IN: NOTORIOUSLY CUTE

Hey-- this had thirteen dollars in it, where did they go?
I'm no detective, but since you're the only other person around, Tbyrd, I'm gonna have to ask: did you take the money?
Um... A little bit.
It is our DUTY as upstanding citizenry of whatever community this is to be good Samaritans!
We must reinstate this currency and leather pouch to the proper duly sworn authorities! To whit: The Constabulary!
I don't know what any of those words you said mean except 'up-standing.' And as you can clearly see, I'm not.
Tbyrd, GIVE THE MONEY BACK.
Okay.
ALL OF IT!
Okay.
TBYRD!
Okay.
Ha! I out-smarted you by yelling! I got allll the money back.
Yep! You sure are observant!

SHERRIF
Hello! I'd like to turn in this lost wallet I found.
WANTED
BANKRO
WANTED
Flim-Flammery
Being Obnoxious
(Within City Limits)
Hmm... Could this guy be that pick-pocket that's been terrorizing the countryside? If he were clever, the police station is the last place he'd think we were looking for him! THAT MAKES SENSE.

WANTED
Flim-Flammery
Being Obnoxious
(Within City Limits)
You're UNDER ARREST!
Sarge will be so proud when I wake him up!
I didn't do anything! I was in Chicago at the time! Oh, you mean him.
Hey!
Hey your own self.
SNAP

Being falsely accused and thrown in jail is the worst.
Psst!
Hmm... there must be a gas leak somewhere.
No! I'm trying to get your attention!
Why? So I can fix the gas leak? I don't have any of the proper equipment!

I'll have you out of jail in a jiffy! Well, more like four jiffies, I'm already kinda tired...
Where did you get that axe?
CHOP! CHOP! CHOP!
FLASH BACK!
Scuse me officer, may I borrow your crime-fighting-axe?
Sure! Wait... Why?
FOR OFFICIAL USE ONLY
For chopping? And um, mystery solving.
Okay! Have fun!
Ta-daa! Finished! Hey Cassowary, I cut a hole big enough so you can escape! Climb thru to freedom! It's better than not-freedom!
Merci, mon-ami! Thank ya laddie!
You're not Cassowary.
Anh-ho-ha! What be yer first clue?
Your moustache. Cassowary's facial hair isn't nearly as luxurious, since he doesn't have any. Also your accent--what is that, Scottish?
Nae, it's French! Yah daftie!
No, I'm pretty sure it's Scottish... You must not know where you're from.

Tbyrd, I'm in this jail cell.
Then who did I just break out?
Me! Henry Hogslice!

You mean Hwafahnrieyee?
No. Say, could I borrow that there hatchet?
Well--
Thanks! Mwahahaha!
ZIP!
Cassowary, I think I may have just done the opposite of a good thing.

Hi again! I lost your axe. Also! How much to bail my friend out of jail? He didn't do anything gruesome, and is a nice guy really.
How much you got?
1 dollar and a hug?
10 dollars and no hugs.

I don't have that many dollars.
I don't want any hugs.

I don't have any money. I mean, I can't find my wallet. Do you have a Lost and Found?
Yeah, come have a look.
Ooh! Found one! It must be mine! Wait, THIS one is mine! Um... They all are?
Wow! You have six wallets?
One for every day of the week!
Where do you put them? You don't have any pants.
I like a nice breeze.
Ooh, I'll take this purse too! And this yoyo is mine. Score, free harmonica!
MEANWHILE...
Oh, Hello. I didn't even see you over there. What are you in for?
Jaywalking.
Moom
Did you know most of your tattoos are spelled wrong?
it's supposed to be ironic.
I have to keep explaining. It makes me cry.
Moom

So, which person do you want to bail out?
That guy. No wait-- I mean, that guy!
Ar-jin-teeeeeena! Don't you cry for meee! Cuz I been from Bally-amma with a banjo for my knee!
Neer neer neeeer nooni nooni noo!
Egads cell mate! That 2 part harmony needs a LOT of work. good thing you're being paroled, you'll never make it in the Jailatorium Acapella Band.
Whew! It feels so good to be on the outside again! The fresh air is delightful!
You were only imprisoned in jail for 20 minutes! I've been locked in suitcases for longer than that.
MANURE

Well, I hope you learned your lesson!
Which?
Don't ever be in the wrong place at the wrong time!
...Um, yes? I won't ever do it again, I promise.

Ooh hey, guess what?
What?
No, go on, guess.
Um... I'm drawing a blank. I can't think of anything.
Spoil sport.
All right! Um, I guess that, er... you are... Darn, my imagination must be broken.
Try guessing something crazy, like 'Am I Smuggling Bunnies In My Hat?'
Oookay... Are you smuggling rabbits in your hat?
Of course not!
That's absurdiculous!
STOP BEING SUCH AN UGLY MUFFINHEAD!
Shh! Quiet up there.
Ding ding ding! Your allotted guessing time is up.
Wait, I was gonna --
I SAID DING! DON'T MAKE ME DING YOU AGAIN!
And the answer IS: I have some left over money!
Yay! We're always broke! How did you get it?
I'm not telling you. You'd make me give it back.

Let's spend the money wisely and responsibly!
Nah! Let's blow it all on one big delicious meal!
C'mon Tbyrd, if we ration this money, it could last us for weeks!
Too late, we've already accidentally on purpose wandered into a fancy French restaurant.
How did I not notice that?
MENU
Hello sir. Good evening madam. Would you like me to be rude and obnoxious? I mean-- tell you today's specials?
Who are you calling madam? I'm not a madam!
Pfft. Heeheehee heehee.
Sir, please restrain your grandmother or I'll be forced to dump champagne on her head and charge you for it.
YOU ARE THE MOST INSULTING WAITER I'VE EVER MET!
Awww! Thank you! Would you mind writing that down for me? I'm trying to win the Maitre D' Society's Annual Prize.

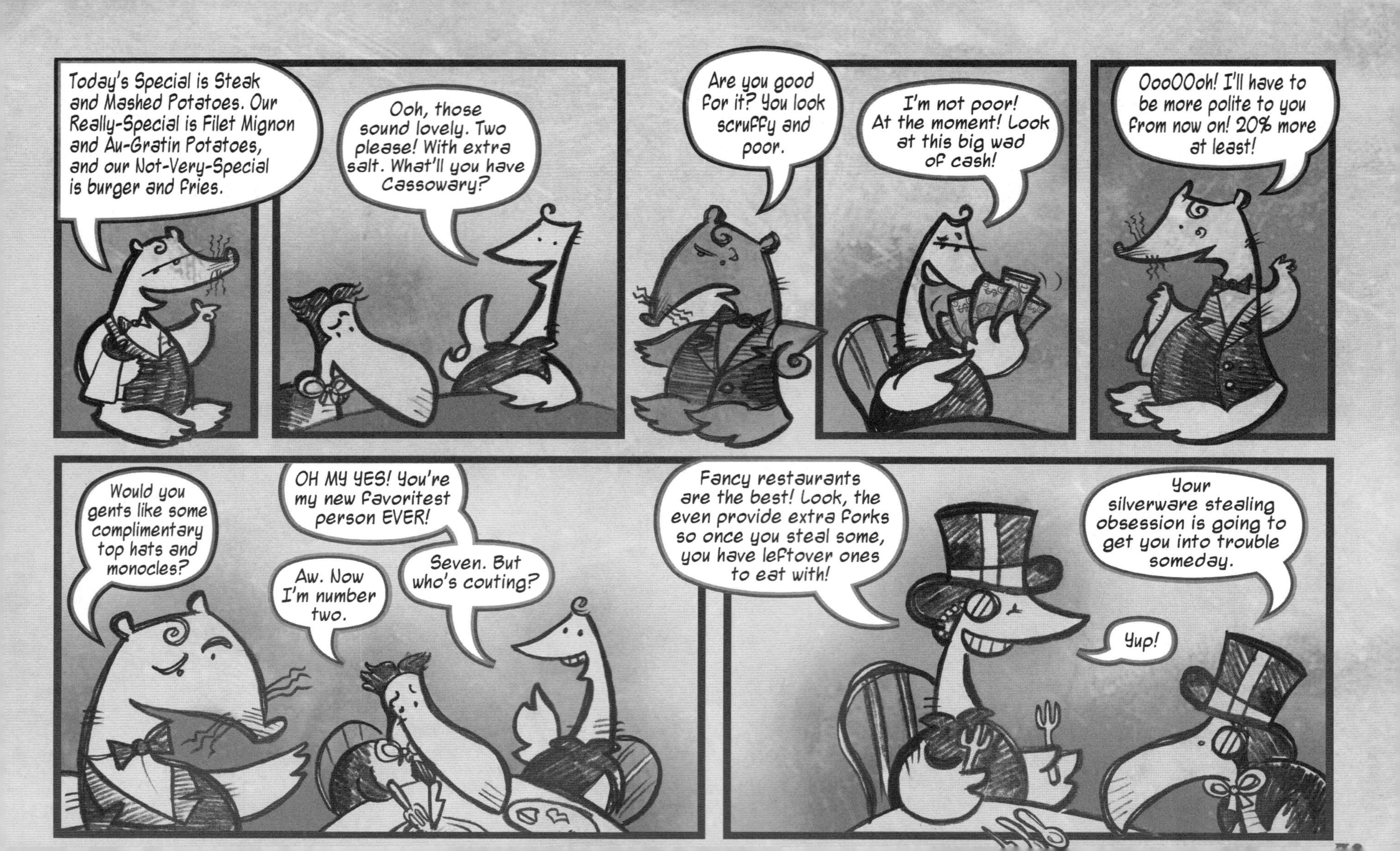
Today's Special is Steak and Mashed Potatoes. Our Really-Special is Filet Mignon and Au-Gratin Potatoes, and our Not-Very-Special is burger and fries.
Ooh, those sound lovely. Two please! With extra salt. What'll you have Cassowary?
Are you good for it? You look scruffy and poor.
I'm not poor! At the moment! Look at this big wad of cash!
OooOOoh! I'll have to be more polite to you from now on! 20% more at least!
Would you gents like some complimentary top hats and monocles?
OH MY YES! You're my new favoritest person EVER!
Aw. Now I'm number two.
Seven. But who's couting?
Fancy restaurants are the best! Look, the even provide extra forks so once you steal some, you have leftover ones to eat with!
Your silverware stealing obsession is going to get you into trouble someday.
Yup!

Hello gents! I'm here to play some music at you! Any requests?
Yes: Go play some-where else.
Ooh, howbout for that ugly woman over there? Something really loud and screechy!
That was pretty rude of you, Cass. Don't like music?
Oh, no, I love music. All my family members play an instrument. I've just never been a big fan of the violin because my brother would always hit me over the head with one. Which is strange, because he played the oboe...
A violin's the same thing as a banjo, right?
No, you're thinking of a fiddle.
I AM NOT! How dare you!
Here's your So-- OOOOOP!
TRIP!
Um... cough. We didn't order any soup.
Well in that case, I'll only charge you half price.
Slurp! Mmm! This soup is good!
And piping hot.
You like? 2/3rds price then! That's my final offer.

So how much are you charging us for the soup you spilled on Cassowary?
Hahahaha! If you have to ask, you can't afford it!
You know, it's impolite to laugh at someone after scalding them.
Do you know, that didn't even occur to me? I'm French, our etiquette is different.
How nice for you. Can I please have a facial towel?
No, we need them all for other purposes.
You're French?
Can't you tell from my OUTRAGEOUS French accent?
This is a comic strip, all the words are written down and you can't read inflection. Try speaking in a MORE frenchy font.
Like This?
No, that's italic.

Tbyrd, I'm more nervous than usual. We can't afford this restaurant!
Pfft. You worry too much.
You don't worry enough!
I have you around to worry FOR me! I'm stress free and content!
I don't want to have to worry on your behalf! I have enough of my own to deal with!
Then stop, I don't care.
But then extra worry will be floating around unaccounted for, harming innocent passers-by!
Serves 'em right!
Don't fret! I finally have a Big-Wad-O'-Money! Everything is fine, and also dandy!
May I see?
Never seen such a Pile-O'-Green before eh? Yeah, it's pretty awe-inspiring.
Hm.
Sorry Tbyrd -- You can't be trusted! I'm stealing this money for your own good!
Zow!

Cassowary! Where are you? I'm bored of wandering around looking for you!
Here I am! I got lost too.
Little buddy! I understand! Heck, I've stolen a friend's TEETH before! That's why I don't have many friends! PLEASE! Gimme the money back!
I deposited it in a bank! So it will be safe!
blink.
blink.
Tbyrd?
Banks? NOOO! AUGH!
AUGH!
Wheee!

Not this bank. A different one.
)gasp!(AUGH!
GLACIER MOOCOW & JONES BANK
You have excellent lungpower by the way.

FRED'S BANK
Okay, we're here. What's the problem about depositing your money in the bank?
Putting your money in a bank here in the old west is the best way to lose it! Nine out of ten banks get robbed by bank-robbing robbers every day!
I couldn't help eavesdropping- Is this a stickup?
No no no! Just a withdrawal.
Do you have an account, or was that a bank robber joke?
Good, because this bank's new 'No Robbing' policy is now STRICTLY enforced.
How strictly?
We have a plaque on the wall, and everything!
NO ROBBING Please
Ooh, with the words spelled correctly and everything! You guys are serious!
We're tough, but fair.

What is your account number, madam?
Seven. And I'm a Sir.

Allow me to enter the information into our typewriter madam.
CLIK
Oops. Typo I hit '6'.

ARG!
I HATE this newfangled modern technology!
CRASH!

Tra la la la la!

Clang!

Ooh! Free typewriter! Score!

Now I can finish my novel!

Why does that keep happening to me?

So, how much money would you like to withdraw from your account Mrs. Cassowunkle?
That's ***Mr Cassowunkle!*** I mean Mr. whatever my real last name is. I would like all of the money please, that $7 of Tbyrd's, plus my entire life's savings.
And can we have it in one of those sacks with the big dollar sign on the side? I've always wanted one of those.
Here ya go!
Seems kinda puny...

It's all there! All $8.47! Minus 5 cents in A.T.M. fees. A.T.M. stands for Arthur Toulouse Moutreck. My friends call me 'Artie', and I like taking fees.

Your life savings is only ***one dollar and forty seven cents?***
Yup!
How long have you lived?

Can we change this $8.47 into pennies so it will look more impressive?
Aw man. It'll take me a while to count out eight hundred and forty seven 'one-cent' pieces.
That's okay. I don't mind wasting your time.
LATER:
844... 846... 847! Done!
Yay!
SWEEP!
FRED'S BANK
Hmmm... This money sack still doesn't seem very full... Hey, gimme a handful of deposit slips, and couple of those free calendars...
There! NOW it looks like I'm rolling in the Benjamins! Or at least some Hamiltons.
But those are pennies! Lincolns!
Gesundheit.
Can we walk past Pongo's Pool Hall on 3rd Street? I wanna impress my friend Nesbit!
...Well, he's really more of an acquaintance than a friend. He's an enemy really! I owe him ten dollars. And I never did give him back his teeth... Nevermind.

Okay then! Let me know if there's anything else I can do for you... Sir.
Actually, one more thing: Do you have any cake?
Tbyrd, *this is a bank,* not a bakery.
I know! I'm just in the mood for cake is all. No harm in asking, what if today's my lucky day?
I have some cookies in my lunch box I suppose I could-- Hey wait! Did you steal my pen?!?
Um... a little bit. I didn't know it was YOUR pen. What kind of cookies?
BANG! BANG! BANG!
Augh! Don't shoot! Jeez, it's just a stupid pen! Here, take it back!
Hi everybody! This is one of those stickups you hear so much about!
Oh... We're just being robbed. What a relief.

Stick 'em up! Hands in the air! Wave em like you just don't care!
Or like you do care even. As long as they're up, we don't care.
See, I toldja! Western banks are always getting robbed! Didn't I tellya? I toldja!
By dastardly flagrant criminal types, yes, I see. Actually, I don't... please stop nudging me in the eye.
Gentlemen! You have the privelege of being robbed by the notoriously cute Quailgunk Sisters! I'm Rita, that's Anna.
No, I'M Rita, you're Anna.
But I'm holding the gun with the big 'R' monogrammed on it!
Hmm. Well now I'm all confused...
gasp!
Tbyrd! I think I've just accidentally fallen in love!
Cassowary, I'm flattered, but you're not really my type. You're not any-one's type really.
No! I mean with those bank robbers! They're breathtaking! I have no breath! They took it!
You called them flagrant a moment ago!
That was before I knew they were women! Plus, they are fragrant! They smell like cinnamon.
Well, no wonder you're holding your breath! Wait, I'm thinking of salmon...

Here, pick up those bags of cash. You're gonna be my hostage and carry them around.
And now to abuse my power... Hit that other muffin head in the face with one reeeally hard.
Sorry Cassowary.
THWONK!
That's okay. I know you only did it because you were told to at gun point.
Um, I might have been tempted to do it anyway, it was kinda funny.
Do it again!
Ow! Being bludgeoned repeatedly in the face hurts! If only some pretty lady would kiss my nose and make it better.
...
...You kiss him.
Hee hee! A catfight duel's abrewin! Fight! Fight! Fite!
Okay, You kiss him Mr Tall, Dark & Smugly!
Um, I've already made it painfully clear: He's Not My Type.

Are you done counting out our dollars yet? We've got 17 other banks to rob today. We're greedy.
thirty-eleven... thirty-twelve... Foo! You made me lose count!
Stop being precise! Just put it in a big pile for us!
No! I have to fill out one of these robbery receipts or else I'm not allowed to let you take the money! Sign here please.
I don't fill out receipts. I shoot them.
BWAMBO!
DARNIT! Missed.
You're a horrible shot! Want me to get a hole puncher and make it look like you shot the paper fulla holes?
Shooting makes me very nervous! And when I'm nervous, I forget things! IT'S VERY HARD TO COUNT WHEN YOU DON'T REMEMBER WHAT A 'SEVEN' IS!

Foo. I'm out of bullets. Anna, trade guns with me.
No! I like this gun best.
They're exactly the same! We bought them as a matched set!
Yeah, but I take better care of mine. I clean it till it sparkles and whisper to it all my hopes and dreams.
FINE. Just give me all your bullets then. It's not as if you're going to be doing any shooting.
I might! What about those flies buzzing around--what if I wish to *destroy them utterly?*
I would swat them for you!
Aw, you're sweet! *And kinda creepy,* but mostly sweet.
Are you developing Stockholm Syndrome or something?
No. I was in love with her ***before*** she took me hostage.
You're not even strong enough to pull the trigger.
Yes I am! I've been working out! Haven't you noticed I've been dropping my gun a lot less than usual?
Oops.
CLUNK!

Out of Bullets + Dropped Gun + Me Holding All The Money = ESCAPE!
EXIT
WHIR
WHIR
WHIR
SLIP!
TRIP!
AWK!
KLOONK!
CATCH?
BANG!

MEANWHILE, AT THE SHERRIFF'S POLICEATORIUM:
Sarge, did that sound like a gun going off, three streets away at Fred's Bank?
Good ears Constable! Mine are full of wax and dirt and stuff. But it was probably just a car backfiring.
Car's haven't been invented yet Sarge.
Oh right. I mean it was probably just a horse back-firing.
Horses haven't been invented yet--Wait...
Let's roll! And don't forget my crime whacking stick.
Truncheon?
Geshundeit.
SEVERAL AMOUNTS OF WALKING LATER--
FRED'S BANK
'Ello 'ello, what's all this then?
Ha! Good one sir!
Thanks! I've been waiting for a good opportunity to use that classic Britishy policemen's line think anyone else got it?
My mother's an English bulldog, so I thought it would be fine. But then, my dad's a French poodle, so I think that cancels it out...
Ooh! We should totally get some crepes after all this!

Officerrrrs! Stop your rambling conversation, and stop these bank robbers! PLEASE!
HEY! Witty banter is an important part of our protocol. We don't tell you how to do YOUR job!
I tell him how to do his job. Whenever I cash my paychecks here, he licks his thumb while counting out my dollars, and I don't want spit all over my president heads!
ANYWAY! Stop all that robberying, or I'll shoot!
Psst: Sarge! You don't have a gun!
They didn't know that!
Um, scuse me officers: I just want to point out that I'm not actually involved in this bank robbery. I'm holding this gun accidentally due to an odd collusion of circumstances. Y'see...
Cassowary! You're the one holding the gun! You don't have to do any explaining!
But I like explaining! It's polite!
You're in control of the situation! You can write your own ettiquette book if you want!
Hmm. Who would publish it?
If you're packing heat, you can get them to print anything you want! I've authored 12 romance novels that way!

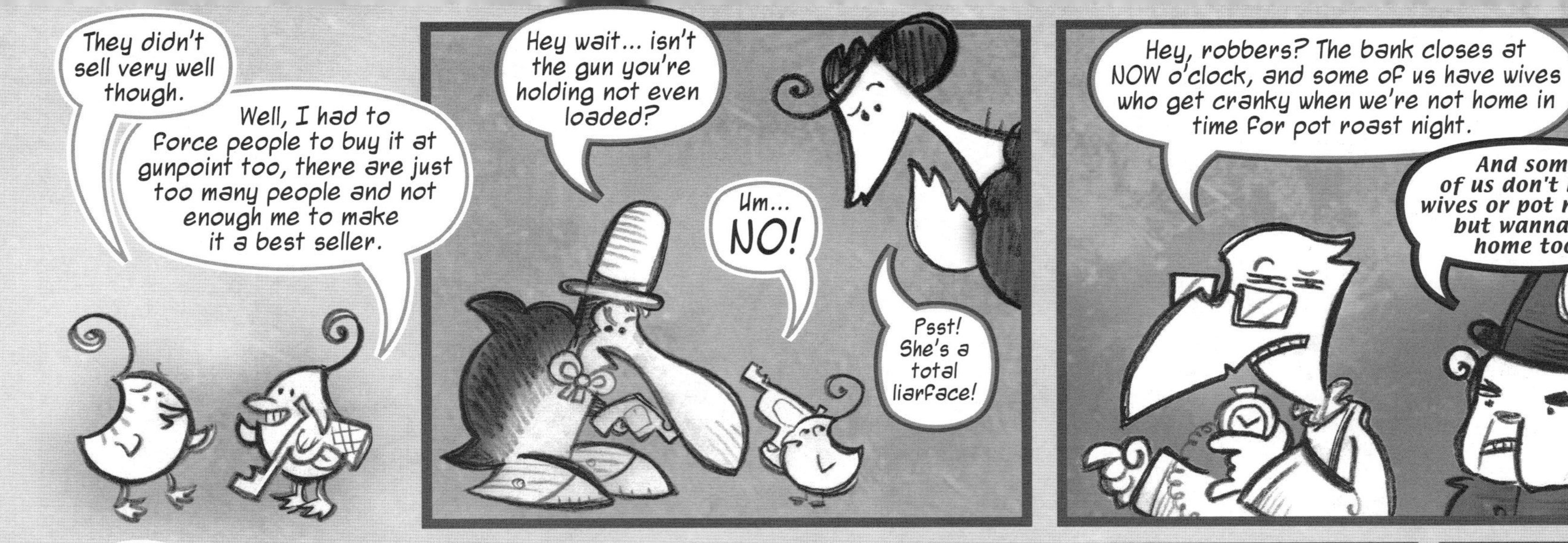

They didn't sell very well though.
Well, I had to force people to buy it at gunpoint too, there are just too many people and not enough me to make it a best seller.
Hey wait... isn't the gun you're holding not even loaded?
Um... NO!
Psst! She's a total liarface!

Hey, robbers? The bank closes at NOW o'clock, and some of us have wives who get cranky when we're not home in time for pot roast night.
And some of us don't have wives or pot roasts, but wanna go home too!

Sorry, this stand off will last till one of us blinks!
I've been blinking this whole time, do we have to start over?

Hmmm...

Smoochy noise!

Woo! My first kiss!
DROP!
CATCH!
Heh. Trickery.

Yay! We won! Let's all go out for a big fancy dinner and celebrate! You guys can be our dates!
Dates/Hostages. But if we find anybody we like better, we're totally ditching you.
Sounds perfectly reasonable! Lucky for you I'm incredibly handsome and suave.
Lieutenant, you go on this date too. The moment they let their guard down, arrest them!
Yessir. Saaaaaaay ladies! Are you the sort of ladies that can't resist a man in uniform?
We can when they have YOUR face.
Ouch.
Sarge! They appear to be immune to my charms! Permission to buy flowers and chocolates?
Granted. Just don't go eating them flowers yourself.
I can't make that promise.
AND SO:
Well! This is nice!
I think we had lunch here...
We had lunch?
But I wanted Chinese.
Too bad! You shouldn't have dropped your gun a SECOND time!

Gentlemen: It occurs to me that there are not enough womens on this date, or to put it another way, too many of us menfolk.
You and Cassowary better fight it out then, winner will be the one who wins. 3, 2, 1... GO!

SCUFFLE!

Boys! Boys! As much as I enjoy being fought over, don't worry about the odd number situation! I'll just have two dates!

Blecch. You can have three, I don't want mine.

So... WHERE ARE MY FLOWERS?

Here! I got you a bouquet of Forget-Me-Don'ts!
um... um! Pass!
I found you this lovely assortment of spoons!
They go great with soup!

Soooo, tell me about yourself.
No.
Okay, I'll tell you about myself.
No.
I don't think this is going very well.
I'm having a lovely time!
Psst! Tbyrd! I've been monitoring your conversation, and I have come to the conclusion that I don't understand these women!
Ouh. That's part of the fun!

AND SO, THE EVENING PROGRESSES, WITH LOTS OF FINE DINING, AND FINE WHINING.
...So, my friend Orongo the Swelligant actually SAWS the lady in HALF! He's not even a magician or anything! He just likes to wear a cape!
Do de doot doot doo dah doo...
Mmm... This parsley is delicious.
Boy, you sure like the sound of your own voice, don'tcha?
I can't tell if your stories are boring or interesting...

Would sirs and madams care for some dessert? We have some cream that has been specially iced!

Oop!
TRIP

SPLURCH

AHA! Carpe Momentum!

Gotcha! You are under arrest!
Hey! Manners? Way to ruin the mood!

Now, I've only got the one pair of handcuffs, so I'll be back to arrest YOU in a minute. Stay right here!
Okay...
My arrest record has doubled! I'll probably get promoted back to where I was before I was demoted!
Sister, you'll come bust me out of jail, right?

I busted you out last time! It's your turn to bust ME out!
PLEEEEEEASE?

Sigh. Okay!

You're tallest, so you get the bill. That's how it works.
Don't we get dessert?
Sir, the other sir is wearing your sir's dessert upon his sir's face. Saaaaay... You seem familiar-- Don't I hate you for some reason?
Mmm! Punkleberry!
An upstanding citizens like me? Probably.
Why you! Hey... Is that a big bag of money?
Yup! And you'll never get your hands on it, I've got you outgunned!
Out-gunned? Ha! You don't know the restaurant business very well!
Oh dear, we're in one of these again...
Hiss!
Grr!
Okay Cassowary, you cover me-- cause a distraction while I run away!
Okay! Then you can come back and cover me while I run away!
Hmm... Something not quite right there...
Ahem! 'Scuse me? If I were to shout "Hey, what's happening over there" would you gunslingers turn and look?
I'd need a REAL distraction, thank you very much!
I'd probably shoot you a bunch accidentally.

I can't believe I'm doing this with a bag of money!
WHAMBO!
SWING!
AUGH!
RUN!
BLAM! BLAM! BLAM!
WHIZ!
Huff! Puff! What a strange day this turned out to be.
It was about normal for me. We're back to square one.
We lost our money, and got shot at! How is that square one?
We got some free meals. That should have put us on square two.
I think we're on square zero.
Stop worrying about squares, we've come full circle! Hee hee hee.
THE END

Is the book over? Are we right-side-up yet?
Yes, and no. Goodbye reader! The book is pretty much done! Hope you enjoyed it!